D1416891

A Dog's Guide to Life

The Bala Diaries

Marc Handelman

Photographs by Michael Winsor

HERODIAS

NEW YORK LONDON

Published by HERODIAS, INC.
346 First Avenue, New York, NY 10009
HERODIAS, LTD. 24 Lacy Road, London, SW15 1nl
www.herodias.com

Manufactured in the United States of America

Design by Charles B. Hames
All photographs by Michael Winsor, except on page 10 (by Rolf Magener)

LIBRARY OF CONGRESS CATALOGING-IN-PUBLICATION DATA

Handelman, Marc, 1963–
    A dog's guide to life / Marc Handelman.—1st ed.
        p. cm.
    ISBN 1–928746–13–6 (hardcover)
    1. Doberman pinscher—Fiction.   2. Dog owners—Fiction.
    3. Dogs—Fiction.   I. Title.
    PS3558.A462525   D64 2000
    813'.6—dc21
                    00–024246

BRITISH LIBRARY CATALOGUING IN PUBLICATION DATA
A catalogue record of this book is available from the British Library.

ISBN 1-928746-13-6

1 3 5 7 9 8 6 4 2

First Herodias edition 2000

A Dog's Guide to Life

Dumped . . . Again!

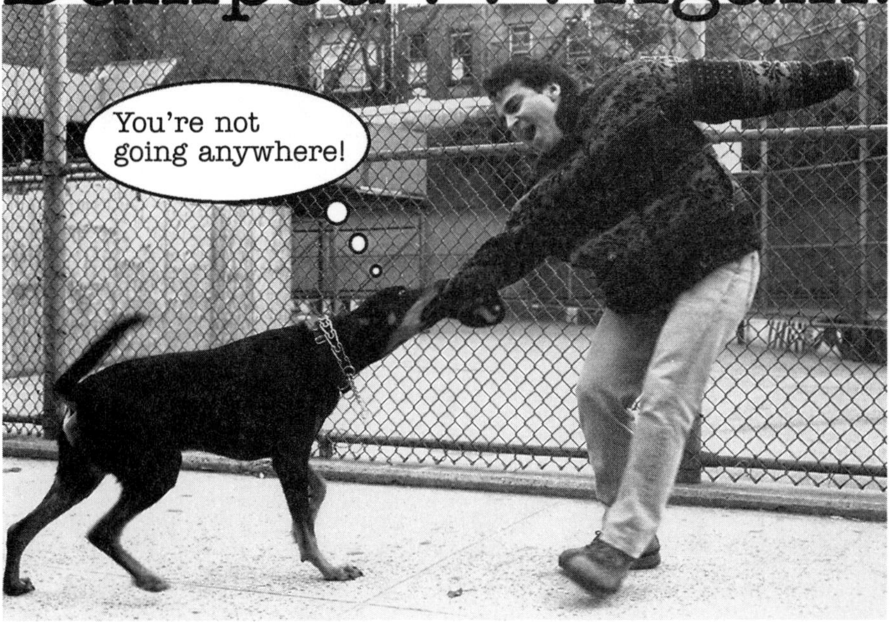

Dear Diary:

I'm a very confused dog. My name is Bala. I'm a two-and-a-half-year-old male Doberman . . . Doberman-mix that is. Half the time I can't tell who's in my pack and who isn't— or who will be there to rub me behind the ears when I get sad. Or who will take me to the park. I get criticized every day for doing even the most natural things. Worst of all, I get Left alone at home for hours. I constantly face the Great Riddle of Dogland: How Not to Get Left.

My new Dad noticed how anxious I was and bought me a rawhide diary from the pet store. He told me keeping a diary is a Good way to feel better—even if I don't have "opposable thumbs" to write with (whatever they are). At this point, I'll try anything.

. . .

Nick, my last Dad, broke it to me a couple of weeks ago. He said he couldn't take me to his office anymore, not after what happened. Worse, he and Aunt Marla were planning to move to a "no dogs" building. What does all this mean? I thought, with my chin pressed to the wood floor. "It means we're going to have to find you a new home, Bala." The shock spread over me slowly, like when you first get in a bath.

You see, the day Nick carried me in his arms from the dog pound was the best day of my life. The pound was an awful place: all those hysterical poodles with drippy brown cry lines squealing "Take me, take me." Panting terriers. Doe-eyed shepherds. Fights over food; mange and lice everywhere; dogs disappearing; new ones coming in; more disappearing. People with Angry Smells pointing and grabbing and prodding. I was constantly wiping away the slobber of a cold, and the rash on my elbow pads from the metal cages was unbearable. And the scratching, Ohhhh, the scratching. I fell madly in Love with Nick at first smell.

And I swore I'd never be abandoned again.

. . .

Nick and I had sixteen beautiful months together. He took me everywhere. He introduced me to all his friends and

Nick, my last Dad

family. He let me run free in the park and in the hallway. He brought me to the drugstore, to street fairs, and to "ATM's." He fed me pizza and didn't mind when I chewed on his shoes. He never got mad at me, even when I ate from the garbage or grabbed his sweater. He was a Dogsend.

Nick even brought me to his "office," a sort of back-up lair where he "made Money."

But then one day I was a bad dog—a very bad dog: I jumped on one of his clients (Okay, I meant it), licked her face (meant that too), pushed her down (didn't mean it), and scratched her neck with my du-claw (didn't mean it!). She ran shrieking from the office. Almost immediately, Nick's partner, Jack, balled up his fists and got a very Aggressive Smell.

Now, Nick, he still had a Love Smell, but he pushed all the papers off his desk anyway. He got all chesty and paced around the room, looking at Jack out of the corner of his eye. "You blew the whole deal, Bala, a major deal!" He wagged his finger at me. "A lot of Money just walked out that door, Bala. Major Money. Do you understand what *major* Money is?"

Given away . . . again.

I sat there with my ears pinned back and my eyes down. To this day, I don't know what Money is (another Great Riddle of Dogland). And Major's the Airedale from 22nd Street.

A few days later, Nick said we were going to take "a little Walk" with two of his friends, a male and a female who live in our building on 21st Street. Suddenly, Nick ran ahead with me and let me off the leash. The female called me from down the block. I ran to her warily, smelling a set-up, since I'm never off my leash in the street. But she nuzzled my nose and scratched me behind the ears and smiled. Then she and Nick made eye contact and nodded. When the four of us got back to our building, Nick sat me on the sidewalk and gave me a big hug. He told me he Loved me very much, but . . . .

Well I'd been through this before, so I knew what he was going to say. And though I'd sworn on a stack of Pizza boxes never to be abandoned again, there was nothing I could do.

Nick handed over the leash.

My New

Mom and Dad

I love my new Mom

My new Mom and Dad are nice. Mom comes when you say "Heidi." She calls herself a "freelance graphic designer." This means she sits alone in front of a humming box the size of a birdcage. This humming box is called a "Mac." When she's not in front of the Mac she plays with small brushes and oil paints and large pieces of paper called canvasses. I steer clear of these canvasses you can be sure: if I even sniff at one, it's *whap!* on the butt with the latest issue of *Art Forum.*

Dad is a "lawyer." For all the world I'm not sure what this means. He is small, as people go, with a full coat of hair on his head and chest and legs. He answers to "Jake." But he also comes when Mom says "boo-bee," which she says when she gets a Spicy Smell.

As I said, Jake and Heidi weren't strangers to me; they lived two floors down from Nick's lair, on the side of the building facing the diner on 8th Avenue that throws out all the Good chicken wings. Jake and Heidi had always petted me nicely, with no trace of Fear Smell. They were Dog People.

We had only been in Jake and Heidi's lair for an hour when they went for their jackets and started making threatening movements toward the door. I absolutely had to impress upon them—in these first moments of our relationship—how serious I was about not being abandoned again. So I sat up straight and tall to show how much I wanted to come. Please put my leash on, I thought. Please, please . . . . I struggled for a way to express my grave concern that if Left alone for any substantial period of time, I'd be forced to chew up some of their furniture, and spread moldy chow mein and coffee grounds all over the nice floor.

Fortunately I didn't have to do any of these things. They leashed me up and took me with them on a long Walk to George's Dog Run in Washington Square Park.

On the way over, I picked up a nice, partially eaten chicken wing on Greenwich Avenue. My last Dad, Nick (now known as Uncle Nick) never minded when I helped myself to food on the street. But my new Mom and Dad reacted differently.

"You'll kill yourself with that bone!" Jake shouted, grabbing my snout in front of everybody, reaching his grubby little choking fingers down my throat, and jerking out the wing like it was his or something. Then, for reasons all his own, he got an Angry Smell. He threw the wing in the garbage.

(Personal note: this could be a problem.)

At the park, there were wooden benches and leafy trees and a view of a huge stone arch. I gotta tell you, sometimes I dream I'm fifty feet tall and I'm peeing on that arch, marking all of New York City.

Inside George's Dog Run, Jake and Heidi sat together jowl-to-jowl on a corner-bench. They held each other's paws and smiled as they looked at each other. They shooed me away to play with the other puppies. Because neither Jake nor Heidi appeared to be in any hurry to run off, I turned, lowered myself to the ground with my butt high in the air, and sprang into action. I nuzzled the other dogs behind the ears. I tug-of-warred with a game bulldog named Max. I ran long, panting laps with a little mutt named Bo.

I played my butt off

14

Before we Walked home, Jake and Heidi put all four paws on me at once and rubbed me up like a big horse. Everything was well in the world. I summoned all the pee I could and sprayed the metal leg of the bench.

This bench is going to be ours forever!

Life in the
New Lair

Dear Diary: My new Mom and Dad have some weird habits. Take Jake. Every morning he gets up and sits on the floor, naked and cross-legged, facing out the window to 8th Avenue. He closes his eyes and breathes deeply. I've heard him say he's "meditating"; personally, I think he's worshipping the diner across the street that throws out the chicken wings.

My response is to sniff his ears. But when my nose gets too close he growls, "noooo," in a low, ominous voice. After a while, he lies on his back and pulls his legs around into positions that appear to cause him great pain. I try to help by bringing a toy for him to play with. But he usually ignores me, and sometimes even makes me Sit and Stay across the room. He really seems to be in pain though. Could it be that people who worship fried chicken are part of some strange, masochistic human cult?

Then Jake gets ready for his daily hunt. At least I assume he's going hunting, though how he would ever capture prey is beyond me. Apart from being kind of small, he doesn't

What is that beeping in there?

have a very keen sense of smell. And he has to put these glass and metal things over his eyes to see. Plus he has trouble chewing on one side of his mouth—a bad sign in Dogland.

An evolved hunter would consider taking a big dog like me along to help. But not my new Dad: He hunts alone, no decoys or anything. All he brings with him is a brown bag which I believe was made from part of a cow. It has a nice jerky taste (I nibbled on it once when they Left me alone). It's filled with pieces of paper and small metal tubes he calls "pens." Maybe they're blow-guns, I can't be sure.

In any case, Dad's success rate on the hunt is shockingly low. He rarely comes home with any food—except for the occasional bag of "cookies." Anyone can catch cookies— they don't appear to be very clever animals.

Mom doesn't leave the lair nearly as often as Dad does, but when she does, she comes back with a kill. I mean, she usually has two, sometimes three full bags of food, including chickens and fish and parts of cows. Dad jokes that her real specialty is catching chocolate ice cream. Mom doesn't think this is funny. I'm afraid to think what would happen if we had to rely on Dad for food.

My new Dad has other crazy habits as well. Before he leaves in the morning, he spends a lot of time in the bathroom. First he puts whipped cream on his face. He misses his mouth completely! Then he scrapes the cream off with a small plastic device. Next he "jumps" into the tub and "takes" a "shower." This is a scary cleaning process involving total immersion in hot water, not unlike a dreaded "bath." There's a lot of steam and the door is closed, offering little hope of escape. It seems to me showering is a crazy thing to do before going hunting since on a hunt you have to be prepared to deal with messy stakeouts, rain, snow, blood, thieving cats—that sort of thing. Why would anyone clean themselves before a hunt?

One good thing about my Dad is that he farts a lot. He's a powerful farter, too, which is great because the stronger they smell the easier it is for me to remember what they smell like. His best ones come after eating a small animal called a "burrito," which a short, greasy-smelling man brings to the door after Mom and Dad finish arguing about who should cook. Mom always asks who farted, and Dad always says "Bala did." I don't understand why he's so quick to give me credit for his excellent smells.

But the best thing about my new family is that Heidi stays home a lot. She sits in front of her Mac and makes clicking noises with this little thing she calls a "mouse" (I smelled it—it was no mouse). The Mac hums and makes other bizarre sounds (even when she's not there!). For hours my Mom stares at her Mac and moves her fingers around on the buttons—tap, tap, tap . . . tap, tap, tap—and the pictures change and change and change. Then she yawns and rubs her eyes so hard I think they're going to come bouncing out onto the floor. Finally another box with little flashing lights whelps a piece of paper that looks like what was on the screen. Pretty impressive.

Today she told me she was "designing a logo for some Wall Street guy." She said it was what she had to do to make Money. Like I've said before, I don't know what Money is, but watching what people will do to get it, I'm not sure I want to know!

Though she spends most of the day making these "logos" and other things called "ads," Mom says she really wants to do something else. Specifically, she wants to do "Art." It's almost like "Arf," which means "hello, I'm over here," in Dog. Dad laughs and says, "Fine, but if you do Art,

I get to do Art's girlfriend." Mom calls him a dog when he says this. I wish.

Along with art and Dad, Mom also Loves "cappuccino" (a word that puts me in mind of an Italian dog with a hat on). In reality, cappuccino is a drink that helps humans move more effectively from one task to another. Mom's always asking Dad to fetch her these cappuccinos. He runs out for a moment and returns with her drink. It's one of the few hunting exercises he's good at.

Anyway, when I think Mom has made enough of these logos and ads, I put my paw on her arm and she makes nice to me.

One way Mom makes nice is to clean my ears. (I have lots of ear wax.) But instead of running me off to the vet like other Moms, she sits there with cotton swabs and cleans and cleans and cleans. She says, "Ooooh, look at all that dirt," and kisses my head a lot. Mom understands that cleaning is the highest expression of Love in the animal kingdom. Dad doesn't seem to understand this.

Unlike Mom, who (with the help of cappuccino) stays on task very well, Dad returns from the hunt and rushes

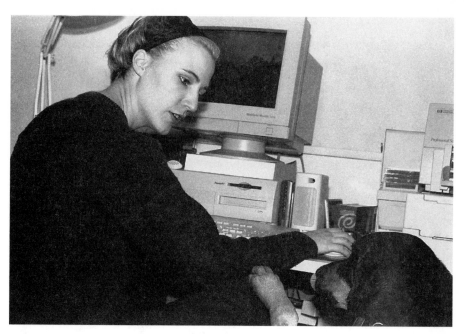

Pay more attention to me, Mom.

senselessly from one thing to the next. He either "shoots baskets" (I didn't realize they were such a threat), "goes running" (though I can't say from what), "writes" (on his own little Mac), or "reads" (a rude process that involves propping a ream of paper between his cheek and my kissy face).

Yes, dear diary, reading is definitely Dad's most annoying habit. Today he was reading a book by someone named "Froyd." I put my head in his lap. "Excuse me," he grumbled, "but I'm developing my mind."

Okay, Dad is the Alpha Male in our pack and everything. And I have nothing against Froyd. But hey, what about abiding the ol' Pleasure Principle once in a while and playing with me? Plus Dad should be developing other things beside his head, which is big enough already (at least according to Mom). His nose, for example, could use a lot of work; I know for a fact he can't smell his way in the dark. Plus he's always complaining about tooth pain. And his upper body is, as I've said, rather puny. I recommend he get a big stick and play tug-of-war with me three times a day to build up his arms.

Come on, Dad. . . . Don't wimp out now!

When he's finished reading, Dad often takes Mom Out, leaving me alone in the lair. I try to explain to my Dad that Mom doesn't need to go Out, that she takes care of her business quite well in the bathroom. But my Dad just doesn't listen.

At night, he finally slows down. But by then it's late, so when I come up to him with a toy and put it on his tummy (hint, hint), he ignores me or yawns with sleep. It's all I can do to get him to throw the thing once or twice.

But then, out of nowhere, he gets a burst of energy, and he and Mom take off all their clothes and make their wrought-iron bed shimmy and shake the lair. The whole thing gives off a very Spicy Smell, and they don't want me doing any cute pack things like laying across their legs or cleaning their noses. They yell at me to go away, and then become very strange and possessive of each other. It makes me feel that they don't Love me anymore. As a full member of this pack, I'm going to have to see where this leads.

My
Neighborhood

Dear Diary: We live in Chelsea, a neighborhood in New York City. A lot of people think the city is no place for a big dog. But that's a myth. While Chelsea may not have a lot of grass, and there are only a few trees, it makes up for it with a huge dog population. You can smell "dog" everywhere: parking meters, the bottom steps of brownstones, car tires, garbage cans, and, of course, hydrants.

One of those dogs is my girlfriend Friday. She's a beautiful, pure Doberwoman, with her ears cropped all nice and sharp. She lives on 19th Street with "Florence," a pale-looking woman with bad skin and a bunch of metal rings in her body that look like they must hurt a lot. Whenever we meet on our Walk, Dad and Florence let Friday and me play. Friday and I get along better than any other dogs I know.

I wish Friday and Florence would join our pack and come live with us. But that's not going to happen. You see, Dad is averse to forming a bigger pack. "I'm not ready to have a baby," I heard him tell my Uncle Nick (though from

My Gal Friday (on the far left)

what I understand of human biology, it would be Mom who would be doing the heavy lifting).

Me? I think it's Good to take in new pack members; we dogs frequently take in strays who need homes. But when Dad and Mom see a stray person rummaging for food and needing a good cleaning (like Luther, the Man Who Lives Outside), they pass him right by. Which leads me to believe that dogs might be more evolved than people.

Car alarms also brighten my Walk. They go off at least once a day, and at night, a lot more often than that. While Dad covers his ears and steams, I enjoy the rhythmic pulse—boo-wee, boo-wee, boo-wee, an-an-an-an-an-an-an-an, weow, weow, weow, weow. . . . The sound reminds me of a primitive pack call, a warning that intruders may be near. Keeps my instincts in shape.

One thing about Chelsea is that there are always girl-girl and boy-boy couples strolling arm-in-arm, making nice to each other. Dad refers to these couples as "gay." Hmm. I thought "gay" meant "happy." Does this mean male-female couples like Dad and Mom aren't happy?

I was pondering this on our Walk when we came upon the Chow-Chow named Sing. Now anyone with half a nose can tell that Sing and his kind are very territorial. So, instinctively, I menaced him. I can't let that blue-tongued fur ball think he owns 21st Street! Anyway, a strong Fear Smell rose off Dad and he grabbed me by the collar and choked me half to death. "That Chinese butcher would kick your candy ass, Bala. Don't you know they fight mountain lions?"

Actually, I didn't know that. But what Dad didn't know was that the day before, my girlfriend, Friday, presented herself to Sing, which tipped my water bowl real good. So when I saw Sing today I growled and made like I was going to put the ol' choppers on him. I would never have bitten him, though. I don't bite.

I'm a Lover, not a biter

Sex in the City

Dear Diary: Went to George's Dog Run again and quickly established dominance over our favorite bench. Mom cocked her head back in the sun. Dad positioned a bunch of newspaper in front of his face and read.

Friday was there. We nuzzled each other, ran a couple of laps, and play-wrestled. I was having so much fun that all of a sudden I found myself snaking my way up her back, sticking it in, and moving my hips back and forth. It wasn't planned; it just happened.

Dad yelled at me to get off, but my hips just kept on chugging—sort of like I'd seen Dad do with Mom! It was the most natural thing in the world. But then there was a *whap!* of newspaper on my butt and a violent tug on my collar. The metal spikes dug in and Dad pulled me across the park with my paws dragging. I was very confused, since Friday liked it!

Dad made me Sit and Stay and then he apologized to Florence, who thanked Dad for pulling me off. Dad told her there was no need to worry, since I had been "fixed." (I didn't know I was broken.) What a double-standard: I mean, Dad and Mom can spice up the joint any old time they like. And I can't even try it once! Friday and I are mature adults now. It's Dogscrimination, I say!

Then Dad and Florence started talking and laughing and making nice and Dad even got a little Spicy Smell going himself. But Mom went over and looked at Dad funny and got an Angry Smell and Dad's smell changed right quick and he got all flushed. Mom then abandoned him, stalking off to another part of the dog run. Dad didn't like this at all.

We left the dog run and Walked to another part of the park. Mom told dad she thought they should "talk." Dad said he didn't see what there was to talk about. Mom said that was typical: that dad never wanted to Speak to her when she was upset.

"I Speak to you plenty!" Dad said. "Well then Speak!" Mom yelled. "I could see what was going on between you and Florence." Wow, I thought: Mom commanding Dad, the Alpha Male, to Speak! I listened attentively to see how this early challenge to Dad's authority would play out.

Listening to humans communicate
can drive a dog crazy

Dad sheepishly asked Mom what she meant. Mom said he knew exactly what she meant—that a woman could "sense" these things. "What things?" barked dad. "Come on!" she squealed. "You were getting Off on that bimbo!" Dad insisted he wasn't getting "Off" on anything.

Which was true. I know what "Off" means. And I didn't see Dad get Off anything. (Except our bench. And that was to *whap!* me in the butt with the paper.)

"Heidi, can't you just Drop It?" he pleaded finally. "No!" Mom fired back. "No I won't Drop It." All very curious, since there was absolutely nothing in Mom's mouth to Drop! This exchange confirmed once again, dear diary, that the biggest problem facing humans today is their inability to communicate.

Sundays in
New York City

Dear Diary: "Sundays in New York" are special for my Mom and Dad. But I don't get Sundays at all.

For one thing, the word "Sunday" is a total misnomer, since the sun comes up every day.

Also, Mom and Dad brag about "sleeping in" on Sundays, though I've never seen them "sleep out." Of course, I like it when they sleep in. It means we get our longest group-cuddle of the week. After which Mom lets Dad paw at her and the two of them get all Spicy again. (Now I just leave and sulk in the other room.)

After we get out of bed, we go to "brunch," an orgy of food eaten among total strangers, any one of whom could come right over and steal from our plates. Mom and Dad found a sidewalk café that permits me to sit quietly beside them while they eat. This is one of the best things about Sunday: I don't get Left at home.

To me, meals are supposed to be a time of joy, but not brunch. First, Mom and Dad discuss some soon-to-be-former friend who gave Mom or Dad the "brush off" the night before at a party or in a bar. Personally, I like being brushed off.

Then there's a fight about what to do for the rest of the day. Mom usually wants to see "modern photography," while Dad wants to go to "the Met" to see "the masters." I don't see why Dad, an Alpha Male, needs to see other masters.

Unlike at home, they discard a lot of food at brunch. I mean, *they hand it right back!* And after that Dad usually carps about all the people (not to mention the dogs) who are "starving." One of those people is the man from our street, Luther (who's also known as "homeless"). We frequently see Luther pawing at thrown-out pizza boxes and gnawing hungrily on sharp pizza crusts and chicken wing bones. Why not take the extra brunch food to him?

Sundays are also distinguished by the shockingly large amount of newspaper that appears in our lair. The first time I saw this pile of papers I thought: I haven't seen so much newspaper since I was a pup! Perhaps they've invited a huge litter of puppies over to pee on the floor. (Naw, couldn't be.)

They always say they're going to read these newspapers. But more often than not the papers sit around "cluttering up the place and getting ink on everything" (Mom's words). When Dad isn't looking, she takes the papers down to the basement.

Every fourth Sunday or so Mom and Dad stay home. These Sundays are known as "laundry" days. In fact, Laundry Day may be its own day in the human schedule of things, like Monday or Friday. On Laundry Day Mom and Dad sort and bag and fuss over their clothes. I help as much as I can, usually by jumping into the middle of the pile and lying down. "Off!" says Mom. "We're taking those to be cleaned." I do get Off, but it always depresses me, since I like the way the clothes smell after Mom and Dad wear them for a couple of days. What does it say about their self esteem if they don't like their own smells?

Beware of Neighbors

Dear Diary: In addition to various Dog People (like Uncle Russell and Aunt Jamie, who let me jump up on them and explore the garbage pail in their apartment), we share our building with some real mutts.

One of them is the "Drunk Woman from Down the Hall." I don't know what "drunk" means. But I've noticed she always smells of the bottled liquids that Dad and Mom only drink on the weekend. Because of this smell, people pass her by as if she were covered with bleeding puss-wounds. The smell's not *that* bad.

Anyway, the Drunk Woman is very chatty. When we meet her in the lobby she grabs Dad's forearm and leans close to talk. She Speaks very loudly, even though she's close enough to lick my Dad's ear. She wants Dad to tell her whether her ex-husband will "come up with the Money," and if there's any way to avoid the new tax on cigarettes. (Like many humans in our neighborhood, she eats these burning fire sticks constantly.) Dad listens patiently and answers the best he can.

One day the Drunk Woman knocked on our door. She was shaking and her face was streaked with salty eye liquids. She had a piece of paper that said they were "throwing her out for not paying rent." Dad let her inside and brought her a drink. He read the piece of paper and assured her she wasn't going anywhere; that it would take them years to kick her out; that a Good lawyer could keep her in her apartment practically forever . . . .

The Drunk Woman asked if Dad could be her lawyer!

I looked at Mom, working away in her office, then pressed my snout to the floor and moaned quietly. I still don't know what a lawyer is. But whatever it is, Dad must not be one for other females! He's Mom's lawyer and that's it! Fortunately, Dad told the Drunk Woman he couldn't be her lawyer. He told her to call "beagle aid" instead. (Though I find it hard to believe a small hunting dog with a hoarse bark and a very long tail could be of much assistance. Perhaps I misheard.)

The Drunk Woman clung to Dad's arm; she really wanted *him*, she said, not some stranger. Dad gently shook himself free. He would give her "behind the scenes" advice, he said. But that was it.

The Drunk Woman loosed a steamy exhalation. "It's about Money," she said, "isn't it?" Dad nodded. She agreed she couldn't pay Dad since, she chuckled, "I drink all my money." (Well, that explains that.)

The Drunk Woman helped herself to another drink. Then she sat down and proceeded to tell us her entire life story—how her mother and father died and how she had to live with some uncle in Montreal who took her to bed and made her bark like a dog. At which point she went, "rrrrr, ruf-ruf, ruf, ruf-ruf-ruf-ruf, rrrrr," which means: "I'm going to pick up twenty-five chicken wings and go voyaging with your blood enemies." She said it quickly and with a French poodle accent, but I'm pretty sure that's what she said.

Then the Drunk Woman closed her eyes. Her breathing got louder and she began to slouch further and further into our couch. She spilled her drink on one of Mom's art magazines a second before Dad's hand reached her glass.

Dad quickly woke the Drunk Woman and ushered her into the hallway. "Crazy polluted lunatic," he muttered as he cleaned up the mess, all the while looking over his shoulder toward Mom (who sat Nicely in front of her Mac, blithely unaware). Then Dad ran outside and returned with a dry copy of the magazine. Luckily, Mom didn't notice the difference.

Another one of our neighbors is The Man Downstairs. He came up a few days ago. At the door I licked his hand. It tasted all right. Nothing great, but all right. Mom, however, had a Cautious Smell. Sure enough, the man told Mom I make too much noise when I Walk, and that if Mom didn't put down thicker carpeting or something he was going to complain to the "super," whoever that is.

Well, you don't have to be Underdog to know that I have very, very thick nails and that when they're not on Mom and Dad's bed or the couch, they're on the floor. What am I supposed to do? Sprout wings and fly? Mom and Dad Walk around the house, don't they? Why didn't The Man Downstairs complain about them? In fact, Mom and Dad and their old neighing bed can make quite a racket. Sounds like more Dogscrimination to me.

Mom agreed. "Go ahead and complain to the super," she said. "I'm not going to Roll Over for this."

A lot of females would have Rolled Over. But not my Mom! She'll stand up to any male! Even Dad.

I wish I could be tough like my Mom and not have to Roll Over . . . .

The Great Riddle of "Money"

Dear Diary: This morning the three of us were Walking together when we saw Luther, the homeless man, sitting against the wall outside the diner. He was eating chicken wing bones right out of the trash! I waited for Dad to react—since he often speaks of "helping the homeless."

C'mon Dad, I thought, watching Luther crunch the bones. This poor man is about to render himself paraplegic, perhaps even kill himself! But Dad didn't reach down the old man's throat or anything; he just pushed right on through.

We were a few steps past the old man when he said, "I need Money . . . I'm seventy years old and homeless . . . can you help?"

Mom pulled Dad's hand forward, but Dad paused, reached into his pants and came out with one of those green pieces of paper with the picture of the guy who looks like an ice cream cone. He handed it over to Luther. I noticed Mom made a lip-sucking sound.

Is that what Money is? Just a piece of paper? And, if so, how is it going to help Luther? He can't eat it. And it's too small to be used as a blanket.

Later that day, Mom went Out and came back with a big new table for our lair. I sniffed it for a moment: yecch! It had that alcohol-smell that humans insist on putting on natural wood products. "Don't even *think* of chewing on it," she said.

Later, Dad returned (empty-handed as usual) from his hunt. He stared at the little table. Mom was sitting on the couch with a mug of cappuccino. She explained how we now had a place to put her Beanie Babies. She observed how the table "further defined the space." She looked closely at Dad for a reaction. He nodded slowly and said nothing. Suddenly the air became thick with tension. Finally Mom sighed. She said she "knew that look" and what was the matter? Then she answered her own question.

"It's the Money, isn't it . . . ."

Dad used some words I've never heard, like "credit card balance" and "chapter eleven." He told Mom not to forget that he worked in the public sector (wherever that is). He added that we weren't "made of Money." And that Money didn't "grow on trees." Duh-uhh.

Mom said, "Why, if Money is so tight, is it okay to give it away to that Luther guy?" I couldn't see for sure, but I think my Dad's hair stood up straight on his back. But before he could say or do anything, Mom began gathering her Beanie Babies, one of which fell onto her cappuccino, spilling it all over the place.

"You win," she snapped.

Dad shuddered as if he'd taken a bullet. And as Mom stomped away, dripping cappuccino on the floor, I couldn't help but notice that Dad didn't have a Winning Smell at all.

Mom took the table away the next day.

Dog's
Best Friend—
A Dinner Party

Dear Diary: In an attempt to get past their Money conflicts, my Mom and Dad decided to throw a dinner party. They invited Uncle Nick and Aunt Marla, and Uncle Russell and Aunt Jamie. I Love dinner parties. With Mom and Dad focusing on the company, the chances of getting People Food increase dramatically.

. . .

Party day! After much cajoling from Mom, Dad stopped reading and went out on an afternoon hunt. He was gone for hours, but all he brought home was a roll of paper towels, a box of crackers, and a few bottles of red liquid which Mom said were the wrong color. He also picked up another book by Froyd at the Strand Book Store.

Mom accused Dad of taking care of his own needs instead of helping out for the party. And though there was still cleaning to do, she went on a supplemental hunt— alone. She was gone for just a few minutes, but she humiliated Dad again, bagging a tub of "hummus," all manner of farm-fresh vegetables, two bottles of clear liquid, and several good-looking salmon. And she didn't even get wet!

I stood watch over the food as Mom resumed poking around on counters and tables with her trusty cloth, dusting and wiping in long strokes. Dad watched for a moment, mumbled something I didn't hear, and opened one of the bottles of wrong-colored liquid. He asked Mom if she wanted a drink but she said no. Dad drank like he'd been voyaging for days.

I was relieved when the party started, and I planted myself in front of Uncle Nick with my shoulders back and my head held high. Have you ever heard of Divine Intervention? Well, there's also a thing called Canine Intervention. Canine Intervention is when you're sitting by the kitchen table and an Invisible Dog causes a piece of food to fall off someone's plate.

Sure enough, at dinner, Uncle Russell accidentally fumbled a forkful of salmon; I caught it before it hit the floor. And Nick was so happy to see me he just put some rice in his hand and held it down. Two slurps. Gone. "Guys, please!" Mom said, kneeling to kiss my forehead. "I don't want Bala gaining any extra weight." Uncle Nick said "ooops," and Uncle Russell said "Okay, Bala, no more." But when Mom and Dad weren't looking Nick and Russell slapped palms under the table. Nick and Russell are Dog People.

"You treat him like a human child," Aunt Jamie observed.

Mom said I *was* her child. Jamie sniffed. Didn't Mom "want to have 'real' children?" she asked. "Isn't having children the reason we were all here?" The clinking sounds of forks and spoons ebbed and then stopped. Dad and Mom exchanged a look.

"Being creative and doing art," Mom said, "are why Jake and I are here."

Jamie countered that having children was the highest form of creative expression.

Uncle Russell started to get an Anxious Smell. "Jamie, chill out, OK?" "No," Jamie said in a loud voice. "No, I will not chill out." Jamie was starting to sound and smell like the Drunk Woman from Down the Hall.

Dad thumped his glass down: "Jamie, you have to admit that writing and painting are just as creative as child-rearing!"

"My children—if I ever find a man good enough in this horrible city—might change the world!" said Jamie. Mom calmly said her paintings might change the world too. Uncle Russell just squeezed the bridge of his nose and sighed.

I was sitting there thinking how nice it was to see my Mom and Dad defending each other, like real pack members do, when suddenly I was overwhelmed with the sad realization that I had caused the whole fight! It had been about me! About whether I was a human child or not!

For a while, I struggled with this existential point. Mom feeds me and cuddles with me and cleans up my business, right? She teaches me to Walk nicely (to "Heel"). She talks to me in English until I understand. She takes me out to play. . . .

Was I my mother's son? I felt that I was!

After a troubled silence, Aunt Marla told Jamie and Russell and Mom and Dad to lighten up and let each other choose their own lives.

Aunt Marla was right.

Dear Diary: Like any dog, I try to spend as much time in bed with my pack as possible. And, as with any pack, what happens in bed has a lot to do with whether a relationship succeeds or fails.

Getting in bed with Mom is easy. Mom, you see, is very, very sleepy in the morning, and if Dad so much as paws at her once (except, perhaps, on Sundays), she growls and Rolls Over. At which point Dad gets out of bed—my cue to hop up and curl in next to her.

But when Dad's still in the sack, getting in bed with Mom isn't so easy. When the bell alarm went off two mornings ago, I did what every dog does when he hears a bell: I salivated. Then I jumped up for a cuddle. Dad must have been tired, because he turned the bells off and fell back to sleep. So there we were, lying together like a real pack, drifting off into a few moments of bliss, when Dad suddenly lurched forward, slapping at his shoulder as if a big bug were biting him there. In fact, I had drooled on him.

"Bala! Off!" he said, alpha-maniacally.

I snorted with displeasure but got Off. This was an example of what was fast becoming our worst double standard: I mean, you should see the amount of drip and drool my parents leave on the bed.

Lately, Mom and Dad haven't even been liking each other in bed. Last night when they went to bed I sat outside the door and listened. The bed began to neigh as usual. But all of a sudden it stopped. "Lift Your Leg," Dad said. "No," Mom answered. "Come on, Lift Your Leg," Dad repeated. "I'm not a machine!" Mom said. "You have to try something new once in a while."

Gee, Dad, I thought helplessly, if she doesn't have to Lift Her Leg, she doesn't have to Lift Her Leg!

Dad then asked what he should do instead. Mom told him he was the man; and that he should take charge for once in his life and chart a new approach.

Dad didn't breathe for a while. Then he stalked out past me and into the living room. He lay on the couch with a Sad Smell, watching TV. After a while Mom got a Sad Smell too and came out and sat next to him, stroking his head like she strokes mine and cooing "boo-bee,

I brought Dad a toy to cheer him up.

boo-bee" over and over. Soon the Sad Smells became Spicy Smells and they went back to bed. I was happy, but worried.

Cleanliness is Next to Dogliness

Dear Diary: The subject of cleaning is a big source of disagreement for Mom and Dad. I'll confess right here to occasionally contributing to the problem.

For instance, when Dad comes home, I run to greet him and clean him and otherwise pay tribute. I lick his nostrils, nibble his earlobes, and nose about in his chest hair.

"How come you don't make nice to me like that?" Mom asks.

Boy, Mom is not too bright sometimes. I mean, Dad may be visually challenged and a little small, but he is the alpha male—and as such, commands a certain amount of respect. He reminds Mom of this fact, but Mom disagrees. She says that if anything, *she's* the alpha male. I've seen Mom without clothes on and this just ain't so. Look, I don't play favorites: Dad's got the balls and that's that.

(This is a sensitive area for me, since I don't have balls anymore, a great personal mystery.)

Anyway, getting back to cleaning—they clean me well enough (in the tub with warm, bad-tasting water), but they can't ever agree on how to clean the lair. For example, Dad plays basketball and leaves his socks to dry on the floor. Mom yells, "I know you were never much of a nineties man, but this is the new millennium, you have to pick up after yourself!" Dad grumbles, then dutifully hangs up his socks. Of course if it were up to me, he would leave even more of his clothes on the floor; they smell like my Dad; I like to lay on them when he leaves.

Sometimes a mess just can't be helped. A few days ago Mom got up with Dad and began packing a bag. Dad packed one too. Then they Left—together!—with nothing more than a pat on my head and the old, "We'll be back soon" lie. I looked out the window and watched them move down the avenue. Where were they going with those bags?! How long was I going to be here?

I was so upset, I threw over the garbage pail in the kitchen and dragged the bag into the living room, trailing smelly milk cartons and coffee filters with old grounds all over the house.

When they returned, Dad looked at the mess, chased me from room to room, then beat me on the rump. I poked my

Wait! Where are you going with that bag of clothes!?

nose into their bags (gym bags, it turned out, which now smelled of sweaty clothes). I tried to communicate why I lost control. But Dad wasn't listening to any excuses. "You can't even go to the gym without this idiot dog trashing the house!" Now how are we going to get these coffee grounds out of the carpet?"

"The vacuum," said Mom.

The worst was today. I woke up not feeling well and got sick on the carpet in the living room. Dad mumbled that I must've eaten a cheese wrapper or cigarette butt out of the garbage (lies! lies!). Grudgingly, he started cleaning up the mess in the dark—one wipe and that was it. I tried to point out the spots he missed, but he was in a hurry to go on his hunt.

When Mom got up and found vomit on the floor, her Angry Smell was thick. "I do all the cleaning around here. It's just not fair. Now there's a spot on the rug for the rest of our days on earth." She used more Angry words and I went under the bed. Then she went out shopping for a special cleaning fluid, came back, and cleaned for a long time. All this before she even had her cappuccino!

How Not to
Get Left

Dear Diary: I'm coming close to solving the Great Riddle of How Not to Get Left. When Jake gets home from his hunt, I lie across Mom's lap and pretend to be asleep. For a while it worked. Then—darn it!—he took her away anyway. "We're going out to eat," he said. "You be Good." He's a lying dog: there's plenty of food up in the cabinet.

I don't get it. We're so happy as a family. We like to lie on the soft carpet with our arms and legs all looped like a real pack. So why does Dad always insist on breaking us up? I wish I could get my Mom on my side on this, but she seems to like leaving too. She makes complicit woo-woo-woo noises in Dad's ear when he comes home, and then next thing I know is—slam!—and they're out the door.

Now everyone knows that human children hate to be abandoned. When Left alone, they will sometimes destroy things. "Spite-work," people call it. Very natural behavior—no reason to call in the specialists. Well, it's the same for dogs. Today when they Left me I chewed up one of their magazines.

It's hard for Mom to leave if I lie on her lap

Mom went rabid. "That was the pet catalogue!" she screamed (did she mean *dog*alogue?). "I was going to order you a coat for winter."

This did sound like a problem at first. But then it occurred to me that I still had my good black-and-tan coat. And my original paw pads should get me at least through next winter, and possibly a lot longer.

Let's face it, getting Left is no fun at all. The first dog who can write a book explaining how not to get Left will become very famous in Dogland.

My Dad the Writer

Dear Diary: Dogs Love to search for things. For me, it's usually a bone or a tennis ball.

Well, it's no different for people. My Dad, for instance, has been searching for something he calls "happiness." His unhappiness seems to arise from his dealings with "lawyers," whom he refers to as "unethical bastards." I've also heard him refer to them as sharks. Perhaps one of them bit him.

Lately he speaks of combating his unhappiness problem by "working at home," where there aren't any lawyers. He wants to devote more time to "writing his novel," which is about these odious, unethical lawyers. He says he's going to "get them back" in his book. Yeah, right.

When Dad is "writing his novel,"his fingers move around really fast on a tiny humming box of his own. Yesterday he was working away when I decided I needed some Love. With a blue pull-toy in my mouth, I placed my head on his thigh. "Not now Bala," he said, without looking up. I whined softly. "Not now!" he screamed.

I know my Dad Loves me . . . even if he yells sometimes

Fine, I thought, stretching my rump out and sliding my paws forward on the floor to lie down. But there was an odd rubbery tug under my paws and next thing I knew the thick black cord I'm not supposed to chew on was out of the wall.

The humming from Dad's box stopped. His jaw dropped open. He gave off a fierce Angry Smell and he whacked his open hand against my butt. "Get Ouddahere!"

I scrambled to my feet as he slapped his hand to his forehead and turned his face to the ceiling. "You turned off my damned computer. If I've lost any of my novel I'll beat your dog head in!! (I was under the bed at this point.) "I can't believe what I have to put up with here!" he yelled.

I can't believe what I have to put up with here either.

Anyway, while Dad's hatred of lawyers is real, I don't think he's ready to stay at home with us yet. This morning, after stretching, breathing, and chanting in front of the window, he Rolled Over on his back and called to me. He hugged me and said he had "smelled the coffee" and that writing fiction was crazy. There's no Money in it.

I thought if there's no Money in writing, then that was a plus for writing.

After a while he spread out his arms and legs and lay very still, breathing slowly. I tried to cheer him up by (surprise!) putting a ball and a pull-toy on his belly, but nothing worked.

The Problem
with Religion

Dear Diary: There's a problem gnawing at the foundation of our pack. Mom and Dad refer to this problem as "religion." As near as I can tell, it has to do with one's belief in who created people and dogs and chicken wings and fire hydrants and the like. This need for certainty—that one religion tells the correct story of creation—must spring from the allegedly more developed forebrains of humans. I can assure you, dear diary, that dogs could never dream up an idea this divisive.

Apparently, human views on the question of Creation vary widely. From where I Sit, though, it's all pretty simple. I was created by two dogs, at least one of whom was a Doberman. Chicken wings come from chickens who were created by other chickens. Hydrants grow out of the ground, obviously, and people? Well, who can be sure where they come from?

Ours is what people refer to as an "interfaith" pack. Mom's a Catholic and Dad's a Jew. (I'm not sure what I am, though Dad refers to me as a Zen Bone-ist when I'm chewing a bone for a long time).

I've heard Dad say that neither he nor Mom "practices" religion. Perhaps that's why they're so lousy at it—I can't say for sure. In any case, they were both unprepared for what took place last night.

Two older people came up for dinner. They smelled a lot like Dad—as if they were all members of the same pack. They even looked a little like Dad. Sure enough, Dad introduced them as his Mom and Dad!

The Moms circled each other warily, and I noticed a Cautious Smell—the kind my Mom sometimes gets when Dad is around other females. Dad's Mom then handed over a small, wrapped box.

"How nice!" Heidi said, opening the box. "It's . . . it's . . . it's a lighter!"

"No," said Dad, smelling for all the world like a dog facing euthanasia. "It's not a lighter; it's a *mezuzah!*"

Mom and I didn't understand the Hebrew word. Dad's Mom (whom I shall refer to as Grandma) explained that the mezuzah was for the outside of our door—a sign that a

Jewish family lived there. A very powerful Anxious Smell then rose from my Mom.

Dad quickly offered to fix drinks. Dad's Dad ("Grandpa") endeared himself to me by requesting "Wild Turkey." I snickered like Muttley, knowing full well that Dad wouldn't be able to track down even a domesticated turkey on such short notice. But, lo and behold, he returned and handed Grandpa a glass of turkey stock that the older man drank in one gulp. I could only guess that my Dad had captured, liquefied, and secretly stored an actual wild turkey at some point. Very prudent.

Dad drank his drink in one gulp too, then brought out the food. He and Mom had prepared tuna steaks. Grandma tasted the tuna. She chewed very, very slowly. Every one watched her. Then there was a long discussion about how long and in what juices Dad had or hadn't "marinated" the thing.

I sat nice and tall with my chest out, hoping to get a little piece of tuna (lack of marination not being a real problem for me).

"Doesn't he sit nicely?" asked Grandpa, breaking a long silence.

"Like a big Buddha," my Mom said. "Hey!" she said to Grandma, "Did you know that Jake's doing yoga now?"

Grandma seemed to take a piece of fish down the wrong pipe.

"Yoga? Now it's Yoga?"

"It's really just a lot of deep stretching," said Dad, kicking Mom under the table.

"*Oy vay,*" said grandma. "With the chanting too?"

Dad nodded.

"My son the Buddhist."

Dad couldn't contain himself. "What's the matter with Buddhism?"

Nothing, I thought, during the silence that followed. And if becoming a Buddhist means sitting peacefully on the floor near an open window worshipping the smell of chicken wings wafting up from the diner, then count me in too.

"So what's with this *mashuga* business?" Mom asked when my grandparents left.

"*Mezuzah*," corrected Dad. "*Mashuga* means 'crazy.'"

Mom said mashuga was what she meant. She asked if she was going to have to convert. Dad said he hadn't really thought about it, and that Mom shouldn't jump to conclusions.

Mom didn't jump anywhere. But she did retreat to the bedroom and slam the door.

As usual, I was very confused. I had met both sets of parents. Each came with the same complement of smells: Cautious, Anxious, Sad, Angry, Happy, Spicy, Winning . . .

Why . . . why do people torture themselves with artificially created differences?

The Beginning
of the End

Dear Diary: Things went from bad to worse after the battle over Religion. After a silent Saturday breakfast, Mom went back to bed with the covers over her head—a signal she needed "to talk." But instead of going to her, Dad left the lair to "shoot baskets." When he came back later, the fight was on. I just hid under the bed and shook as the Angry and Salty smells grew and grew. They were screaming, growling and shouting.

I feared a kill.

Well, fortunately, there was no kill, but Dad did punch and break a tall glass container. Dead flowers and water everywhere. Mom then grabbed the books from Dad's shelf with both hands, hurling them around the house. For a while, Dad pawed at his books, picking them up and letting them fall. It was kinda sad to see him that way, a sightless, defeated old alpha male, sighing over his dusty books. Then he let himself out for a Walk.

While Dad was out, a strange human appeared. He was a male, taller than Dad, and much stronger, especially in the paws. Mom led him to the humming box in her office, pushed some buttons and a piece of paper came out. The Stranger said it was the best he'd ever seen and that he would have the coolest letterhead of any trader and how was he ever going to thank Mom?

Mom said, "I know how!" and, to my great surprise, she lay down on the floor on her stomach and jiggled her shoulders. I started to get a little short of breath. The next thing I know, the Stranger straddled her from behind and began rubbing and kneading her shoulders and back. I thought I was going to have a heart attack.

"You have amazing hands," she told him at the door.

When Dad returned, I noticed that he didn't smell Mr. Amazing Hands on Mom's clothes at all. Bad teeth and a poor sense of smell. A dangerous combination. Not that I'm going to challenge Dad or Mr. Amazing Hands or anyone else. But I am handsome, and I do have great teeth and a wet, active nose.

Anyway, Dad and Mom haven't smelled Spicy or made the old bed neigh since the battle over Religion. This has made everyone sad, but no one more than Mom. She talks

Bala

on the phone to her friends about how she's not sure if Dad's "the one." She says her "clock is ticking" and she wants to have a family before it's too late.

I thought we *were* a family.

This morning we were lolling about in bed when she sprang it on him: yes, she told Dad, she wanted to have a baby, and soon. Dad stared at her as if she'd grown a tail.

"Oh boo-bee, you don't even want to get married," she said, beginning to cry.

Dad held her close. He told her she hadn't called him boo-bee for a long time. She said it was because she wasn't Happy. He told her he wasn't ready to get married; that he didn't want to rush into things.

Mom said she'd have puppies before Dad was ready.

During the day, Dad spoke with his parents. He tried to explain what had been going on since their visit. He thought it would be important for them to discuss all of their differences during the upcoming Jewish holidays. But Grandpa and Grandma didn't feel comfortable having Mom and Dad over for the holidays, since Dad wasn't taking religion seriously enough.

Tonight Mom and Dad talked and cried right up to the time when the garbage truck picks up the chicken wing bags from the diner.

In the morning they Sat me down for a talk. Mom looked at me through puffy eyes. The Salty Smell was very strong. Her voice kept cracking.

"Bala, your father and I have decided to separate. It's a mutual decision."

"It's for the best" Dad added, forcing goo out of his nose into tissues which, under normal conditions, I would have happily chewed on.

But these weren't normal conditions. And while I wasn't sure what this word "separate" meant, it stank of abandonment—the worst smell of all.

A week later came the Saddest day ever, even worse than when Nick gave me away: Dad abandoned us. Uncle Nick and Uncle Russell helped Dad get his stuff down the stairs and loaded into a big truck. I got to wait in the back of the truck while they packed it with Dad's books and clothes and some furniture. But when it was time for him to leave, they had to pull me out, my paws dragging on the cold metal, my tail between my legs.

After Dad left, Mom cuddled with me and said not to worry, that Dad had "visitation rights," whatever that means.

I was very, very sad. I mean, I could understand if Dad bit Mom or something. Or if Dad went voyaging all the time and came back cut and bleeding and reeking of other females.

But it wasn't anything like that. So I blamed myself, just like at the dinner party when they fought over whether I was their child. It's all because of me! Maybe I'm not Good enough to be their child.

Life just sucks sometimes

Dear Diary: Mom has to go hunting all day now, just the way Dad used to. She says it's to make more Money. Big surprise.

Since Mom's time on the hunt has increased, I spend most of the day Left alone at home. But Dad comes over at lunch time to walk me. I look forward to our short time together. Yesterday he ate a really fine-looking chicken salad sandwich while sitting on the front steps of our building. But right afterwards he got a Sad Smell. He said he Loved me very much and we rolled around on the floor. Then he started saying nice things about Mom, and blaming himself for everything, like I had been doing. I guess I take after my Dad.

I started to lick his nose and lips. He squealed that I was so sweet and nice and how did I get so nice and where do they put all the Love in me and all that other mushy stuff he says. He assumed I was kissing him out of some deep-held empathy for his loss of Mom. What he didn't realize was that he'd left this nice piece of chicken salad at the corner of his mouth and I was just cleaning it off.

I Love you Dad, but a dog's gotta eat.

Lunch time with Dad

Dad came by again today when Mom wasn't home. I was so happy to see him, I wagged a small plant onto the floor—crash! I tensed for a fury but Dad didn't care. He cleaned up the mess (very thoroughly, I might add), then took me out for a Walk all the way to Central Park.

At the park I became entranced with this one spot, so I peed on it and tried to mark it with a stick. It was my way of trying to explain to Dad how important it was to mark and defend one's territory (he still has no idea about Mr. Amazing Hands).

"When have you ever defended any territory?" he asked. "You're like me, Bala, a lover, not a fighter." Then he kissed me a wet one on the nose.

Later, we sat down in the sun alongside a great big fountain and a pond filled with ducks and dented rowboats. I hopped up on the rim of the fountain and looked out onto the pond. I wanted to go in.

"So you can pick off a duck and make a scene?" he said, pulling the choke-chain tight. The ducks were interesting, I'll admit, but I was hot and really just wanted to swim—so I persisted. He exhaled furiously, pulled the leash even tighter

It was time to draw a line in the sand

Dad and I
talk about
the break-up

and took me away. I got all grumpy and started dragging behind and finally just sat down like I used to when I was little.

"Bala, if you're Sad your mother isn't here, all I can say is, you better get used to it." He threw my leash down and stalked away with a wave of his hand. After a few seconds I got the fear of being Left and chased after him. He held and hugged me and soon I was snuffling in his lap like a little puppy. Making up is nice.

Mr.
Amazing Hands
Tightens His
Grip

Dear Diary: Remember Mr. Amazing Hands? Well, he and Mom have been seeing a lot of each other. Seems he has something called a "trust fund." I don't know what a trust fund is, but I heard Mom tell a friend on the phone that "Money won't be a problem for a while." I'll believe that when I see it.

Yesterday, Mr. Amazing Hands came over and cooked spaghetti and meatballs for Mom. He held Mom's hands and looked into her eyes, like Dad used to. Then he said that he and Mom should go to "Florence" for the weekend. I was confused, since Florence is the woman from 19th Street with all the rings in her body—Friday's Mom. Did they really need a whole weekend just to get to 19th Street?

I tried to concentrate on the meatballs, but all the affection was too much for me to bear. For the first time in my life, I left a table with food on it.

The next morning I was up early looking out the window and sniffing the winds for Dad, when Mom came in the room.

"Just like your father used to do," she said trailing the Spicy Smell of rolled-in sheets.

Then Mom began whimpering. Underneath the chair lay a pair of Dad's basketball socks, found (by me) in Dad's old closet. Just then, Mr. Amazing Hands came in and began bouncing a tennis ball right in front of my nose, daring me to play. At first, I didn't move.

"The big lug must be Sad we can't take him to Italy next week," said Mr. Hands, continuing to bounce the ball.

"He's not a big lug and could you please stop bouncing the ball," said Mom. "You're upsetting him. Look, now he's chasing his tail."

As with many dogs, my tail is a permanent source of aggravation, always an inch or two out of reach. As Mom knew, I tended to chase it when I'm anxious.

Afterwards, Mr. Hands took me for a walk. I hate going for walks with Mr. Hands. He takes me down in the elevator instead of using the stairs (which are home to any number of small pieces of candy left by the neighborhood kids). He always takes me on the same walk, too: up 8th Avenue to 23rd Street, across to the west side of the avenue, back down to 21st Street, across again and home—bor-ing!

During the walk he talks breathlessly into a small hand-held box, ordering pork bellies and coffee and sugar (none of which he ever actually gets). He refuses to let me play with other dogs, even Friday.

But for a guy with amazing hands, I noticed he holds the leash very loosely.

. . .

P. S., I came close to solving the Great Riddle of How Not to Get Left yesterday. Mom was ignoring me, so I decided to nose around in one of her bags that's made from a cow. While enjoying all the Mom-smells there, I discovered a smaller bag, also made of cow. It was pretty much bite-sized, so I ate it. The problem was that inside the second bag was a plastic card a little larger than a dog tag and a little smaller than a smoked pig's ear. The card tasted vile but, angry at being Left, I chewed it up through the case and spit it out in little pieces.

Later, Mom said she had to go to Pearl Paint to get art supplies. "I'll be right back," she said, using the second oldest lie in the book ("We'll be back soon" being the oldest lie).

But this time she came right back. "Where's my bank card?" she asked no one in particular. I snuck into the extra bedroom and flattened my chin on the floor, listening as she milled around with an Anxious Smell. It was only a matter of time . . . "Bala! You ate my bank card! I can't go anywhere without that card!"

Hmmmm, I thought. So that's the ticket . . . .

Jealousy

Dear Diary: Dad doesn't come up to the apartment as often anymore; he says he can't handle it. But he came for lunch today. He seemed fine: eating a burrito and farting away. It was just like the old days, me nudging to have the backs of my ears scratched while surreptitiously getting closer and closer to the burrito. But then he leaned his face right next to mine and whispered No. I was thinking how unfair life was—that it was okay for some people to eat burritos and pizzas and hamburgers all the time, but not okay for others—when suddenly the phone rang.

Dad's head jerked toward the phone. He stopped breathing and got a Fear Smell. The phone rang three more times. Then Mom's voice said, "Hi, it's Heidi. We're not in right now. So please leave a message."

Then the voice of Mr. Amazing Hands came on. Dad dropped his fork and stared. The Fear Smell rapidly became a Jealous Smell. Personally, I think Dad should issue a challenge. Mr. Amazing Hands is tall (and he does have those hands), but he's soft in the middle. My Dad could probably whip him.

On Friday morning, Mom and Mr. Amazing Hands left for "Florence." From the way they packed, I suspect Florence has moved to someplace much further away than 19th Street.

Mom arranged with Dad to take care of me. Before Dad picked me up, she told me not to go on walks with him and other females. Mom has nothing to worry about: all Dad does, as near as I can tell, is write and read.

Except for the usual high pile of books and newspapers, Saturday in Dad's new lair just wasn't the same. In the old days, we would lie around like a big pack until almost lunch time. But on this day, Dad got me outside early. We took a walk to the big river where the sun sets and sat out on the end of a pier. Dad brought along a big hollowed-out piece of wood with metal strings on it. He strummed it with his fingers and nice soft music came out of it. He even changed the pitch of his voice and did a little howling at a morning moon.

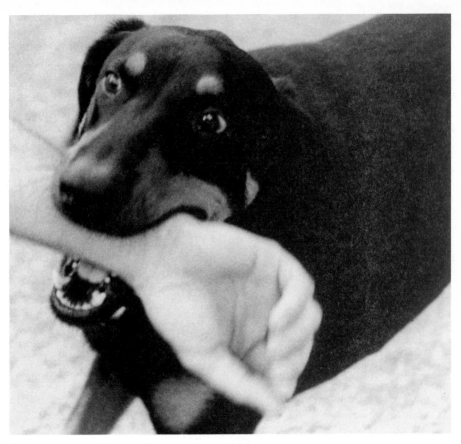

Come home, Dad. Please come home.

We sat there for several hours. Then we went to George's Dog Run, and for a Walk in the Village. As the sun set we returned to Dad's lair to eat.

Mom reappeared on Sunday, so Dad took me home. We met Mom in front of my apartment building and he handed me over. Mom didn't invite him up, which was fine with Dad since on the way over he told me and someone named God Almighty not to let him go up there, that he couldn't bear to set one foot in that apartment . . . .

No Dad, I thought. It's OK to come back. It's OK . . . .

Run for
Daylight!

Dear Diary: The next day, Mr. Amazing Hands came by and took me for an afternoon Walk. We were on the corner of 23rd Street and 8th Avenue, waiting for the cars to stop so we could cross. As I sniffed a metal garbage can, I noticed Mr. Hands had his back turned. As usual, he was yammering into the small box in the palm of his hand. It was time.

I turned around, backed out of my collar, and bounded across the street in five great leaps. Running free was invigorating! I hadn't run on a city street since Nick let me loose to run to Heidi all those months ago. I had a hard time passing Petland on 23rd Street (a Pavlovian Moment), but I forced myself to run on. At the corner of 9th Avenue, I glanced over my shoulder: Mr. Amazing hands was far away, stomping and panting and pumping his arms, an out-of-shape, Money-obsessed fool.

Heading south on 9th Avenue, I felt suddenly weary of my life—of being given away, Left, abandoned, and having my Loved ones disappear. I wondered if it wouldn't be a bright idea to hitch my wagon somewhere else. To get away from these frustrated, pitiful beings who could never be happy—who, try as they might, just can't see the Good. Whose entire lives could be summed up as an endless hunt for a seemingly worthless piece of paper called Money.

As I reached 21st Street, I got a whiff of the diner back on 8th Avenue. I followed my nose and sure enough, they'd just taken out five large black bags bursting with chicken wings and other ready-to-eat foods like cooked egg and bacon. I ripped into the first bag, hunkered down, and was about to munch a nice wet wing, when I heard someone shout: "Money!"

Across the way in the school yard two young humans were bouncing a big striped ball and throwing it up toward a metal rim. Young humans do this all the time here, so, normally, I pay them little mind. Then I heard it again: "Money"! This time, I noticed the ball went through the rim.

Was that the answer to the great riddle of Money—the mere tossing of a ball through the air into a hoop? Still confused, I decided to focus on the chicken wings.

"You're that pretty woman's dog, ain'tcha?"

I hadn't even noticed Luther, the homeless man. He shuffled toward me. I wondered if he was going to try to take some of the food, but he rubbed my neck instead. His paws felt coarse and unclean but there was real feeling there, and absolutely no Fear Smell. I always wondered why Mom was so afraid to let him touch me.

"You want I should take you 'cross the street?"

I looked up at our window, then back at Luther.

"You Momma's gonna be missing you big time."

Again I looked up to our window. Luther was right; mom would soon be freaking out like a dog at the vet. But I wasn't ready to go back, something Luther seemed to understand. I let him massage my shoulders for a time, then I licked his cheek. As I trotted to the corner of 8th Avenue and headed downtown, it occurred to me that in another life, Luther and I could've been pack-mates.

I had a pretty good idea where Dad's apartment was, but for some reason I didn't want to go there. I needed a place to think. And I needed to talk to someone. Someone who wasn't involved. A dogchiatrist.

I went to George's Dog Run.

My friend Bo the Mutt came by, and I told him what had happened. How my Mom and Dad had "separated," and how hard it was. "I want to punish them," I said.

Bo was supportive. He recalled the day his dog-Mom let a strange human take him away to a store in Brooklyn. "Same thing happened to me," I said, and we traded cage stories for a while. Then Bo's master came to take him home. But before Bo Left he said an interesting thing: he said it sounded like I was about to become the first dog to ever not Love his parents unconditionally.

He asked me to consider if that would be Good for dogs.

I sat by our bench and thought about this for a long time. The sun went down and I salivated, since it was dinner time. But my belly was still full of chicken wings and bacon scraps from the diner. It was late when I fell asleep.

I was dreaming about chasing the rabbit, my paws fluttering and body jerking slightly, when I heard: "Oh my baby my baby my baby my baby!" I opened my eyes and wapped my tail slowly against the leg of our bench.

It was my Mom and . . .

. . . my Dad! She was with my Dad!

They reeked of Worry.

Bo provided needed therapy

"Don't you ever, ever, ever run off again, Bala!" they said together. "Do you understand?"

Here they were, the King and Queen of abandonment, wagging their fingers at me for abandoning *them*. It was the final mystery of Dogland: Why humans say one thing and do another.

"Well? Do you understand?"

I understood . . . I understood that my disappearance had brought them back together!

After a lengthy group hug, we Walked back to 21st street, where Mom and Dad kissed and made up and made Nice to each other. The Worry Smells evaporated like steam from the shower. The kissing and hugging went on all night—with me in the bed!

And when the sun began to rise and the garbage truck growled and chomped down on the chicken wing bags from the diner, I finally heard the words I'd always longed to hear.

"Jake," Mom whispered, "I felt so alone without you, so abandoned. Promise you'll never leave me again."

Dad promised never to leave.

And that's when I knew they had finally gotten it.